I sat at my desk and contemplated all that I had accomplished
this year. I had won the hot dog eating contest on Rhode Island.
No, I hadn't. I was just kidding. I was the arm wrestling champion
in Portland, Maine. False.   I caught the largest boa constrictor
in Southern Brazil. In my dreams. I built the largeest house
out of matchsticks in all the United States. Wow!   I caught
a wolf by its tail. Yumee.   I married the Prncess of Monaco.
Can you believe it? I fell off of Mount Everest. Ouch!. I walked
back up again. It was tiring. Snore.   I set a record for sitting i
in my chair and snoring longer than anybody. Awake! I set a record
for swimming fromone end of my bath to the other in No Count,
Nebraska. BLurb. I read a book written by a dove. Great! I slept i
in my chair all day and all night for thirty days. Whew!   I ate
a cheeseburger every day for a year. I never want to do that again.
I trout bit me when I was washing the dishes. but I couldn't catch
him.. w flew over my hometown and didn't recognize anyone. That's h
                                stopped me on the str   said
    was sorry. he sad
me and had the same nam   at are the chances?

THE
GOVERNMENT
LAKE

Also by James Tate

POETRY

PROSE

THE GOVERNMENT LAKE

LAST POEMS

JAMES TATE

An Imprint of HarperCollinsPublishers

THE GOVERNMENT LAKE. Copyright © 2019 by James Tate. All rights reserved. Printed in the United States of America. No part of this book may be used or reproduced in any manner whatsoever without written permission except in the case of brief quotations embodied in critical articles and reviews. For information, address HarperCollins Publishers, 195 Broadway, New York, NY 10007.

HarperCollins books may be purchased for educational, business, or sales promotional use. For information, please email the Special Markets Department at SPsales@harpercollins.com.

Rain Taxi published several of these poems in a limited edition Brainstorm Series chapbook, *The Meteor*, 2016. "Elvis Has Left the House" was first published in *The Paris Review*. Grateful acknowledgment is made to the following publications for permission to reprint previously published poems: *American Poetry Review, Conduit, Denver Quarterly, Fence, Flying Object, Granta, Iowa Review, jubilat, The Paris Review, PN Review, Poetry, Rain Taxi, Tin House,* and *Volt.*

A hardcover edition of this book was published in 2019 by Ecco, an imprint of HarperCollins Publishers.

FIRST ECCO PAPERBACK EDITION PUBLISHED 2020

Designed by Suet Chong

Library of Congress Cataloging-in-Publication Data has been applied for.

ISBN 978-0-06-291472-9 (pbk.)

20 21 22 23 24 LSC 10 9 8 7 6 5 4 3 2 1

CONTENTS

"I sat at my desk and contemplated all that I had" is the last poem James Tate wrote, found in his typewriter as he left it. The poem was originally published in *The Paris Review*, in its fall 2015 issue; a limited edition broadside by Guy Pettit for Flying Object was printed on the occasion of James Tate's Memorial Celebration, January, 2016, New School, New York.

• • •

Love and thanks for insights and essential help in so many ways to Brian Henry, Kate Lindroos, John Emil Vincent, Guy Pettit, Emily Pettit, James Haug, Earl Craig, and Matthew Zapruder.

THE
GOVERNMENT
LAKE

ETERNITY

Wild poultry inhabit these hills. Nobody knows how they got there or how they survive. They just do. Oh sure, a fox picks one of them off every now and then, but they can fly short distances and they can peck like crazy, too. Of course hunters hunt them as well. And they are not very hard to hit. But they multiply quite rapidly, so it all works out for them. Lose one, gain three, and so on. How they get through the winters is a mystery, but they do. Feathers started drifting down our chimney. They covered the kitchen after a while. They got in our food. Mildred complained of a stomachache, and after a few days she laid an egg. We were quite astonished and didn't know what to do. She sat on it for a few days and then it hatched. It was a cute little chick, and it resembled Mildred in certain ways. She sat on it for a few weeks, and then we let it roam the house. A few weeks later the same thing happened. Mildred had a stomachache and a few days later she produced another chick. Soon the house was filled with chicks and Mildred was giddy with delight. I was bewildered and didn't know what to do. I was feeding them all the time and cleaning up in between. Mildred had no time for me at all. She was chasing her chicks day and night. The house was filled with feathers no matter how much I swept. Then one night a fox got into the house. I don't know how. It happened so fast. There were feathers everywhere. And in the shortest time there were no chicks left and the fox had disappeared as quickly as it had appeared. Mildred said, "What are we going to do? There's nothing for us to do now." "We'll go on as we did before, when there were no chicks," I said. "But I can't imagine that. Without chicks there was nothing," she said. "Without chicks we had one another. We loved each other, remember that," I said. "It seems like so very long ago," she said. "To me, it seems like it was only a few days," I said. "To the chicks it was an eternity," she said.

MY NEW PET

It was Thanksgiving and there was no one on the street. I was down-
town and nothing was open. I was alone as no one had invited me to dinner.
I had no family nearby. It's not that I hadn't friends. It's just that
they had forgotten me. I walked along the streets, not feeling sorry for
myself, in fact rather happy just being alive, when I noticed that a
dog was following me. He was just a mutt, but rather sweet looking. I
stopped to let him catch up with me, and then I started petting him. He
seemed to like it. We started walking together. When we got back to my car
I picked him up and put him in. I drove out to my house, which was barely
in the country, just three miles from town. I let him out and went inside.
He wagged his tail and ran around the house exploring. I went into the
kitchen and made us some hot dogs and baked beans. I put his in a bowl
and called him to dinner. We ate at the dining room table, the dog right
beside my chair. When we finished I grabbed the dishes and washed
them. Then I went to take a nap. The dog jumped on the bed
and lay down beside me. I decided to call him Snuggles. We slept for an
hour, then got up. I found a ball and started tossing it to him. He
brought it back every time. Then I had to do some work. I settled down
at the table and opened my notebook. I concentrated on the problems I had
for an hour or so when I noticed Snuggles wrestling with a three-foot black
snake. I couldn't imagine where it came from. Snuggles was tossing it in the
air. Then, suddenly, the snake had wrapped itself around Snuggles' neck
and Snuggles was gagging. I jumped to my feet and grabbed the snake as hard as I
could and yanked it free and smashed it to the floor. The snake crawled away

into my bedroom, but Snuggles died right there in my hands. I laid
him down on the couch and went looking for the snake in the bedroom, my
new pet.

INTO THE NIGHT

Sister Bodie walked out of the church. She looked around, grabbed her chest and fell down. Several parishioners gathered around her. One knelt down and picked up her head. That was Brother Paul. He said, "Sister Bodie, the Lord loves you." She said, "I know, Paul, I know." And with that, her head went limp. The crowd sighed. Then she rose up off the ground above the crowd and hovered there for less than a minute. Then she burst into flames and came sifting down in ashes. Paul stood there shaking, speechless. Sister Ruth said, "It's a miracle! What are we to do?" Brother Eric said, "Stay calm. Nobody do anything. We've got to figure this out." Sister Eileen said, "I think she went direct to heaven, without bothering even to go to her grave." Brother Paul muttered, "Yes, I think so." "Let's sweep up her ashes," someone said. "No, don't touch them," said another. "Why?" someone asked. "They might be sacred," Eric said. "Maybe she went to hell," someone in the back of the crowd suggested. Those surrounding him started to beat on him. "Let him alone," Brother Eric said. Paul started to cry. Sister Eileen offered him her hanky. "Let's sing," Sister Ruth suggested. They started to sing "What a Friend We Have in Jesus." When they finished someone said, "That was the most maudlin version of that song I've ever heard." They looked up and there stood Sister Bodie under the oak tree. They all gasped and Brother Paul nearly fainted. Sister Ruth said, "How did you get here?" Sister Bodie said, "Church is over, ain't it?" Brother Eric said, "But you're dead." "Which of you fine gentlemen is going to walk me home?" Sister Bodie said. A stunned silence fell over the crowd. Finally, Sister Bodie said, "Well, how about you, ladies?" Again, silence. Brother Paul said from the back of the crowd, "I'll walk you home, Sister Bodie." "I knew you would," said Sister Bodie. And so the two of them walked off into the night, though it was barely noon.

THE SEAHORSE

My pet seahorse was acting sick this morning. He must have eaten something that didn't agree with him. I thought of taking him to the doctor, but couldn't find one who would see him. I looked up seahorses in a medical textbook and it suggested mouth-to-mouth respiration. So I reached in his aquarium and pulled him out. I placed my mouth on his and put my thumb and forefinger on his abdomen and started breathing on his mouth. I squeezed my thumb and forefinger back and forth as I breathed. After a while I started to fill with gas. I looked down and my body had grown enormous. I started to rise away from the seahorse towards the ceiling. I bounced around until I finally went out the window. I rose in the sky and floated around until I went to the sea. I started to lose altitude and crashed in the waves below. I started swimming towards shore. A boat came along and picked me up. The captain asked me what I was doing there so far from shore. I hated to tell him the truth, but I did. "A seahorse breathed in my mouth," I said. "You're lucky to be alive. That's a terrible thing, there's nothing worse," he said. "But he was sick. I was trying to save him," I said. "He was faking it. He was just trying to lure you in," he said. "Really? I feel so stupid," I said. "Well, at least you're alive. A lot of great men died like that. Jesus, Napoleon," he said. "Jesus? Jesus died breathing the breath of a seahorse?" I said. "Sure. They had to cover that up, of course. That wouldn't do for the savior of mankind," he said. "I don't feel so bad now. Thanks for telling me," I said. "Oh, you're in good company, all right," he said.

THE PRAIRIE DOG TOWN UNDER ATTACK

Hereafter the little dogs of the prairie shall be known
as Peter and Rob. Oh, and Martha and Anne. And then there were
the little ones, Larry and Katie and Artie and Frank and Jamie
and Barbara. I'm sure there were more. They moved around so
fast it was hard to tell. Anyway, Bob was out scouting for food
one day when he met a wolf. They started talking about food
when the wolf suddenly looked at Bob and said, "You would make a good
snack for me, you know that?" "Oh, no, I taste like poison. You
wouldn't want to eat me," Bob said. "I've had one of you before. You
don't taste like poison. As I recall you were delicious," said
the wolf. "You must be thinking of my nephews. I know they taste
good, but my tribe tastes terrible and will kill you," Bob said.
"Well, let me just try a leg, we'll see then," he said. Martha
walked up and said, "What's the matter?" "This wolf wants to eat my
leg. I told him it would kill him," Bob said. Peter and Frank
walked up, and Peter said, "What's the matter?" Bob said, "This
wolf wants to eat me, but I told him we were poison." "Oh, yes,
it's a proven fact. Scientists have said it's so," Peter said.
"Just a bite won't kill me. Come on, don't be afraid," the wolf
said. Katie walked up and bit the wolf's leg. "Ouch," the wolf
said, "that hurt." "See what I mean, and you aren't even poison,"
Peter said. The wolf reached and grabbed Katie and gobbled her
down. "We'll see who's poison," he said. The prairie dogs all
gathered together. "You're going to die," Peter shouted at the

wolf. "We'll see about that," said the wolf. The prairie dogs
all charged the wolf and started snapping at any part of him they
could get at. The wolf jumped and twisted in the air and screeched.
They wouldn't stop. The wolf reached out and grabbed Bob and
swallowed him whole. Peter backed off and cried for a few minutes.
Bob was his best friend. But then he charged the wolf and jumped
and bit him on the nose. The wolf cried and backed off. He coughed
and hacked and eventually he threw up Katie and Bob. They were all
right and ran to join Peter and the others. The wolf had had enough
and turned and ran away. The prairie dogs were so happy they didn't
know what to do. "Man, it was dark and grizzly inside that wolf,"
Bob said. "I rather liked it in there. It reminded me of before I was born,"
Katie said. "I'm just glad to have you both back. It wasn't the same
without you," Peter said.

PARTNERS

I was at work when Jane came into my office and said, "You'll have to do this over again. This draft is a mess. It's full of errors and misquotes. The way you describe the poundage is all wrong and we'd never get it home that way. Really, Craig, I don't know what you were thinking." "I was just trying to get it here as fast as possible, that's all, Jane," I said. "Well, it certainly didn't have to go through China. You must have lost your mind for a while," she said. "China seemed like the shortest way, and, besides, there's no tariff there," I said. "The hell there isn't. There's a 1,000 percent markup there. Everybody knows that. You're living in the dark ages. Get with it, Craig," she said. "It works for me. I'm sorry if you feel that way. Maybe you had better get another partner," I said. Jane went over to see the boss for a moment. When she came out, I went in. When I came out things were silent for a while. Then Jane blew up. "Can nobody see what's in front of their face?" she screamed. I said, "Oh, shut up, Jane. You think you're the only one who works here. You're an outcast, really." "Oh, go to hell, you big fat slob," she said. "You're a skinny weed of a woman," I said. "Don't get personal with me. Let's keep this strictly to do with work. You have fucked up something terrible. You're about to sink this whole ship if you don't turn it around immediately," Jane said. "You're so dramatic. I haven't done anything wrong and you know it. If we'd just do it my way you'd see," I said. I went to the

coffeemaker and poured myself a cup. She went to the bathroom.
When she came out I had my feet up on my desk. "You stink,"
she said. "I have on my favorite deodorant," I said. "I can't
believe you sent that through China," she said. "It'll be here
tomorrow," I said. The boss walked out of his office and stared
at us. Then he spoke. "I've been listening to you two fight
all day. You haven't done any work, and I can't get anything done.
Therefore I'm firing you both. Clean out your desks and get out
of here." We were stunned. We thought we were working.
When we had cleaned out our desks we stood at the door
looking at each other. Finally I said, "I love you, Jane."
And she said, "I love you, too, Craig." "Would you like to go get a
drink with me?" I said. "I can't think of anything I'd rather
do," she said.

DEBBIE AND THE LUMBERJACK

I'm sorry I never said goodbye. I'm sorry I forgot your
birthday. I'm sorry I ever met you. I'm sorry I bought you
that drink and made you sick. I'm sorry I couldn't find the way
to the hospital. I'm sorry I couldn't remember what kind of roses
you liked. I'm sorry we fought over such a small thing. I'm sorry
I let the lion get too close to you. I'm sorry I taught you English
all wrong. I'm sorry we flew backwards in a storm. I'm sorry
you never got to eat a meal with my friends. I'm sorry you fell
off that elephant. I'm sorry you never learned to fly. And so many
more things I can't remember or choose not to remember. It's just
that I'm having trouble with the details. Was it you who swatted
me like a fly when I tried to touch you one Friday night? Was that
you who climbed in my window and slept beside me without a word?
Was it you who made the house fall down by simply breathing on it?
We left one day and never came back. We disappeared in the forest
and were never seen again. Someone dragged us out of the bog.
They cleaned us up and made us new again. We walked down the
street as if we had always lived there. We went to parties and
no one knew a thing. We woke up one morning and had our lives
back. I got a job and things went swimmingly. You acted as if it
had always been like this. Then a dinosaur came into our lives.
We fed it and took good care of it. But it wrecked the house
and we had no place to live. We dragged it around for a while.
It ate so much we had to move to the forest. We had no friends and

I lost my job. We thought of trying to kill the monster. Then
one day it wandered off. I accused Debbie of not caring for it
enough. She accused me of the same. We moped around for a while,
not knowing what to do. A hunter discovered us and brought us back
to civilization. I set up a little shop on 14th Street. But
Debbie wasn't happy there. She ran off with a lumberjack and
hasn't been heard of since. I only hope the dinosaur is one
step ahead of them. Or not.

DOUBLE-TROUBLE

I sat by myself at a café downtown. I had a hamburger and a malt.
I had to get back to work in a while, but I had enough time to chat up
the waitress. Her name was Irene and she was from the same nearby town
as I was. In fact, we had gone to the same high school and had the same
English teacher. I liked Irene. She said to me, "Do you ever get home much?"
"Oh yeah, about once a month," I said. "How about you?" "I still live
there. I commute, I guess you could say," she said. "Do you ever see
Bobby?" I said. "Oh yeah, I dated him for a while," she said. "No kidding.
Bobby used to be my best friend," I said. "Is that a fact? We had a vicious
falling out, but I really liked him," she said. "What did you fight over,
if you don't mind me asking?" I said. "Oh, he was seeing another girl.
Marianne was her name," she said. "I used to date Marianne myself," I said.
"It's a small world," she said. "Yes, it certainly is," I said. Then
I hurried off to work. I didn't go back into the café for a week, but when
I did Irene had some big news for me. My divorced mother was dating her
widowed father. We could hardly believe it. It practically made us brother
and sister, but not quite. We could date each other if we chose. We looked
each other in the eye and then looked away. I couldn't go back into the café
for a while after that. It was just too much. I was dating a local girl
anyway. But we eventually broke up, over nothing really, I never did
understand it. She said she wanted more freedom, so I let her go. When I
went back to the café Irene wasn't there. She had quit the previous week
and no one knew why. I asked about her around town, but no one knew anything.
Finally I called my mother and asked her to ask her father if he could help me

locate her. She called me back the next day and said he didn't know where she was, but if I heard anything to please call him. I became obsessed with her and her whereabouts. I quit my job and looked for her full-time. I had some savings which allowed me to do so. I had a tip that she might be on St. Thomas. So I bought a ticket and went there. After searching the island thoroughly I gave up and flew back. That's when I discovered her living in my attic. She said she was sorry, but she just wanted to be closer to me and didn't know how to tell me. I asked her to come down and live with me in my space. She said she couldn't now that our parents were married. It would be too much like incest. "I didn't know our parents were married," I said. "They didn't want anybody to know," she said. "Why?" I said. "In case we got married," she said. "Why?" I said. "It would be too much like incest," she said. "Oh," I said, not knowing what she meant.

ROSCOE'S FAREWELL

The dog played in the snow all afternoon. When we called it in, it was shivering, and it took hours of warm towel rubbings before it settled down. Then it slept like a baby. When it didn't get up in the morning we were worried. Finally my mother went to take its temperature and that's when we realized it was dead. We were all so sad we didn't know what to do. Dad said we should bury it in the backyard, with a full ceremony. So we dug a hole and decided on some scripture to read. Janet picked out some music to play. The next morning we went out to look at the grave and it was all torn up and Roscoe was gone. There were footprints in the snow, so we followed them. They went on for several blocks until we found him playing by a lake with several other dogs. He wouldn't come when we called him. We had to chase him and tackle him before we could lead him home. When we got him in the house he was sweet as ever. We fed him and he cozied up on the couch next to us. We still didn't know how we could have mistaken him for dead. Weeks went by as normal. Then, just as spring was coming on, Roscoe was hit by a car right in front of our house. This time we were sure he was dead and buried him in the previous hole we had not filled in. This time without scripture or music. We just threw him in and covered it up with the old dirt. A week went by and then one day in the schoolyard at recess, there he was, as pert and lively as ever before. I called to him and he came to me. I was so glad to see him I didn't know what to do. My parents were happy, too, though a little confused. We welcomed him home, fed him mightily, and played with him as much as he liked. We thought he might live forever. But slowly we forgot about that and he was just Roscoe our old dog whom we took for granted and barely remembered to feed. He fell ill one day and we didn't even call the vet because, I guess, we thought he would live forever. But he didn't. He died a week later and this time we didn't even bother to throw him in the hole, so sure were we that he would come back to life. We just laid him on the back porch and waited for the miracle to happen a third time. Flies gathered and finally he turned to dust. We swept the back porch as we always had before. Roscoe disappeared forever among the flowerpots and old tin cans, saying goodbye to this world one last time.

THE SKY IS FALLING LIKE BUNNIES

Oliver sat in his chair like milk in a bottle. No, that isn't right. Oliver sat in his chair like a stick in mud. That's not it. Oliver sat in his chair like air in the mouth. That couldn't be right. Oliver sat in his chair like poison in a sandwich. Nope. Oliver sat in his chair like a man on a horse. Not quite. Oliver sat in his chair like a man in a mudhole. Oliver sat in his chair like a pixie on a rosebud. I think that might be it. He bent over and picked up his pencil. Then he started to write. He wrote in a big circle all around the paper, then smaller and smaller until it was just a dot. Then he stared at the dot for a long time until he nearly fell out of the chair. He decided that was a bad idea and stopped. He wadded the paper up and threw it in the wastebasket. Actually, he missed the basket. Oh well, he never was much good at basketball. In high school, he failed to make the team. He looked out the window. It was snowing. In fact, it had been snowing hard for hours. No one was plowing. The streets and his driveway had what appeared to be a foot of snow. Oliver felt paralyzed, he couldn't move. A bunny jumped over his head. Then Beth came into the room. "What are you doing here?" she said. "Just sitting," Oliver said. "What do you mean 'just sitting'?" she said. "That's what I'm doing, just sitting," he said. "I've never heard of anybody 'just sitting.' You must be doing something else, like watching the stars fall or the garbage truck coming up the street or a rattlesnake getting ready to strike, I mean, isn't there anything else in your picture?" she said. "Not really," he said. "Well, maybe you're dead, did you ever think of that?" she said. "I don't think so," he said. "Can you get out of that chair?" she said.

"I don't know. I seem to like it here," he said. "You don't look like you do. You look like you're miserable," she said. "I'm just trying to figure out how that bunny got into the house," he said. "What bunny? I don't see any bunny," she said. "One jumped over my head a few minutes ago," he said. "I don't believe you. You're crazy," she said. "No, I'm telling you the truth," he said. "Sitting in one place too long causes you to hallucinate, that's a proven fact," she said. "Ask the bunny about that," Oliver said. "There is no bunny," Beth said. "Just as there is no Oliver and no Beth," he said. "Now you're getting metaphysical on me," she said. "I'd like to, but I'm too tired," he said. "Wake up! The sky is falling!" she said. "That's not the sky, that's just a bunny I once knew," he said.

A PEA IN A POD

How was I supposed to know where Walnut Street was? I barely knew what town I was in. I drove around for nearly two hours searching everywhere. Finally I found it. Now I only needed to find 347 Walnut Street. I drove up and down the street, but there was no 347. I stopped a mailman and he told me that 347 had been torn down years ago. So I stopped at a bar on Main Street named Teddy's and went in. I asked the bartender if he knew a man named Xavier Butts and he said he did. He washed dishes at that very place and he would be in in about an hour. I thanked him for the information. I ordered a drink and waited. Finally he came in. He was a tall, bearded man with long hair. I said, "Xavier, I'm your brother, Ken. Do you remember me?" "Oh, Ken, sure I remember you. It's been a long time," he said. "We were just kids when they separated us. It's been so long," I said. "I always wondered what happened to you. You were my best friend back then. How the hell did you find me?" he said. "It wasn't easy, I'll tell you. It took me years of searching," I said. "I've got to go to work now. Why don't you go and rest at my place. It's just around the corner," he said. "That would be great. I've been in the car for hours," I said. "I'll see you after work, okay?" he said. "That would be great, I'll see you then," I said. I took his keys and went to his place. His place was a small, modest apartment, but with a nice view of the town. I lay down on his bed and fell asleep. When I woke up he was standing there. "You must have been tired," he said. "I guess so," I said. "Let me fix you something to eat," he said. "Sounds good," I said. "Tell me your story. After our folks were killed in that accident and the court split us up, I know nothing about what happened to you," he said. "Well, my folks were pretty nice, kind of rich. They sent me to good schools, sent me to college. I don't really have anything to complain about," I said. "What about you?" "Oh, my father beat me all the time. I ran away when I was fifteen, never seen him since," he said. "Two peas in a pod," I said. "What?" he said. "Nothing. I feel we're all the same, it's just that the ticking's different," I said. "What's the ticking?" he said. "That's the mystery," I said.

EVERYTHING BUT THOMAS

I walked out of the bank just as I realized it was being held up.
I didn't know what to do, run or hide in the bushes. So, without thinking,
I turned around and walked back in the bank. The thief saw me and said,
"Get down on the ground!" I followed his instructions and got down on
the floor. Then he pointed to me and said, "You, get up. You're going
with me." I got up and followed him. We got in his car and sped away.
We sped past other cars at first, through stoplights, until we finally came to
a parking lot. We got out of the car and quickly got into another, it was
a black Chevy. Then we took off at a normal speed and drove that way from
then on, stopping at stoplights and obeying all the rules. We drove out
past the city limits and into the countryside. If I didn't know any better I'd
say it was a pretty ride, beautiful trees and quaint little cottages. We
drove for about an hour, then pulled off on a little lane and followed that
for another twenty minutes. Then we stopped by a small cottage and got out.
We walked in and turned on the lights. He said, "Sit down." I did and
he got out a rope and tied me up. Then I watched him go about his business.
He took his gun out of his shoulder holster. He made some coffee, he
lowered the blinds. He was nervous, but he also felt good about how things
went. I also felt strangely secure, though I was a captive and tied up.
He looked at me and said, "What are you thinking?" I said, "I feel pretty
good, considering." "You should. Everything's gone as planned so far," he
said. "They don't know who I am and we got away pretty neatly as far as I
can tell." "Good. We'll just hunker down here and no one will find
us," I said. He went to the stove and started cooking up some hot dogs.

He loosened my ropes so I could eat with him. "This is a nice place,"
I said. "Yeah, it was my grandfather's," he said. After lunch he tied me back up.
Then he said, "I'm going to take a nap, alright?" I said, "Sure." And he
slept for a couple of hours. After several weeks together he decided to untie me.
I helped around the house, chopping wood, sweeping the floors, occasionally
cooking something. We were a good couple together. I grew very fond of him.
And I know he liked me. This was our home, and neither one of us ever wanted
to go back. There was a little grocery store about five miles away, and that
was all we needed. We hunted deer and one was all we needed to make it through
the winter. Then one day Thomas got sick. He wouldn't let me call a doctor,
and a week later he died. To my surprise he left me everything, the money from
the bank robbery and the cabin. I stayed on there for the rest of my life,
never marrying, never having children. I had everything I wanted, everything
I needed, everything but Thomas.

O JOSEPHINA

Our little baby, Joseph, was the most precious thing in the world. We took turns feeding him and putting him to bed. Alice couldn't believe how we had produced him. She thought it was a case of divine intervention. She even told the neighbors that. They thought she was either joking or just plain crazy. When he got to be two years old he could talk and walk. He ran around the house like a maniac, and when he wanted to eat he said, "I'm hungry. I want something now. If you don't give it to me I'll kill you." We thought that was the cutest thing in the world. When he was five he started to tear the house down. First it was the drapes in the living room, then he started to kick in the walls of his bedroom. We had to tie him up in ropes to put him to sleep. We had to get him a psychiatrist, who said he was just fine, just a little frustrated that he was the only kid in the household. We tried to have another baby, but it was too late. So we pretended we had another child, which confused Joseph all the more. We set the table for four and pretended to talk to our daughter, whom we called Josephina. Joseph didn't like this at all. In fact, we favored Josephina. We talked to her all the time at dinner. Joseph was sad. He didn't throw things or break them. He just stared into his mashed potatoes as if he wished they and he would disappear. When he entered high school he said he had a sister. Students asked him about her. He said she was very pretty and smart. The boys wanted to meet her. He said she went to a private school. Joseph was a good student and very well-behaved. When he started to date he got very frustrated. He couldn't talk to us at all at the dinner table. His grades started to drop and he was kicked off the soccer team. He got more and more inward as time went by. He said he missed Josephina. He drew pictures of her in his room. It's what we thought she looked like, too. Then one day Joseph didn't come home from school. We were worried sick. By nightfall we notified the police. A week went by, then a month. Joseph was gone. We talked to all the kids at his school. Finally, one girl told us he had run away with his sister. They were in love with each other and planned to get married, somewhere in Nevada where it was legal.

THE JACKDAW'S HEAD

We let them out of prison on Christmas and they never came back. That was okay. We didn't like them anyway. But they did leave a mess. Their cells stank to high heaven. And, it's true, they did commit crimes wherever they went. We felt bad about that. We forwarded their names to other crime prevention agencies in the hopes that they might catch them and put them away in their prisons. But they never did. Crime spread throughout the region. We felt bad about that. Then the leader of one gang became a priest, and that made all the papers. And the leader of another gang started food drives in several poor neighborhoods. Many others joined the army and fought overseas. It was amazing how they had turned themselves around. The man in charge of the prison took full credit for their transformation, though, in fact, he had nothing to do with it. It was the original gang leader, a man named José Torres, who had started the whole change. He said God had showed him the new way. Reporters started looking into it and said he had robbed the church of half its offerings. José said, no, he had taken the money to build another church for elves deep in the woods. The press went wild with this claim, mocking him viciously. José had to quiet down and soon the matter disappeared from the news. One old lady came up to José and said she had been to the new church and it was very nice. José thanked her for her report and said he might need her later if the reporters came back. Three of the soldiers were killed in action in Iraq and José said they might become saints. This got him in trouble with the church seniors and he had to back down. José began to feel that there was nothing he could do that was right. So he left the church and went underground. He dealt in odd trinkets that he had picked up from the church, nothing very valuable, a pig's foot, a jackdaw's head, that kind of thing. Still, the cops were after him for unknown reasons. Then he stopped selling trinkets and disappeared altogether. The chancellor of the old prison was afraid he might try to break back in there. About thirty years later a man in South Carolina claimed to have seen José digging a hole, but it turned out to have been just an ordinary grave, which the man jumped in as soon as he finished.

FISHING IN THE SEA OF GALILEE

I was working in my stall when I saw a rat climb up on my desk. I
was frightened, of course, but I was also ready to do battle. I picked up
my notebook and threw it at him, but he didn't seem to notice. Then I
grabbed my pencil and tried to stab him. He just moved sideways about a foot
and I missed him entirely. He seemed to enjoy this game we were playing.
Then I remembered a Civil War sword I kept under my desk for no particular
reason. I pulled it out and brought it down where he was standing. He took
a hop forward and I missed him altogether. I took another swipe and another.
No luck. I called for my boss. He walked into my office with a .45 drawn.
He saw the rat on the desk, took aim, and blew the creature out of the
universe. Well, that's not quite true. He blew him off the desk and smack up
against the wall where he then slid down onto the floor. "Clean it up"
was all he said before leaving my office. And I proceeded to do just that.
I swept the floor and then got a wet rag and wiped the desk. There wasn't much
I could do about the hole in the wall. When I had cleaned it all up I settled
down to work once more. But I still felt those little beady eyes upon me.
I turned out the charts for next year's production, though I don't think
they were correct. Something about the decimal points seemed arbitrary, wrong.
But I couldn't be stopped there. I plowed on through quotes and catalogues.
When I looked up a rat was staring at me. I called the boss. He showed up
with his pistol drawn. "Kill him," I said. He took aim and fired. I got the
broom and dustpan and set to work cleaning him up. When I had finished I sat
back in my chair and took a nap. When I woke there was a colleague standing
at my door. "Yes, what can I do for you, Henry?" I said. "Would you have a

pencil sharpener I could borrow?" he said. "Why, sure. Let me have a look here," I said. I opened the drawer and there was the pencil sharpener. "Here you go, Henry." "Thank you, Mac," he said. I love it when everything in the office seems so clear and simple. I look back at my desk. A baby Jesus is walking towards me. I pick up my stapler.

THE COW AND THE BUTTERFLIES

I visited my friend Rod who was in jail, I didn't really know what for.
"Rod," I said, "what are you in for? I don't really know what they got you for."
"Oh, it was nothing, just screwing a cow," he said. "What in the world
would make you do a thing like that," I said. "I was lonely," he said.
"But still . . ." I said. "I know, it sounds like a pretty sick thing to do
but you'd have to put yourself in my shoes. I hadn't seen a woman in over a
year," he said. "Where were you?" I said. "On an island. It was a dairy farm,"
he said. "Where was that?" I said. "In Iceland," he said. "And what were
you doing there?" I said. "I was working," he said. "Still, it seems like a
very odd thing to do," I said. "It was. I regret it. I must have been crazy
to do a thing like that," he said. "I guess so," I said. When I got home
I visited his mother who was in a nursing home. She asked about her son
and I said he was doing just fine. Then we talked about her life there.
She said she missed her cat most of all. He used to wake her in the
morning and now she forgets to get up altogether. But her keepers make sure
she gets her exercise. And the food isn't too bad. She likes the pudding they
serve. She said I should visit her daughter sometime. She lives on
Long Island. I said I would if she would give me her address. She did,
and the next week I went there. Marjorie was surprised to see me. She lived
alone in a little cottage. She served me tea and soon we were talking away.
She wanted to know all about Rod and I lied again. I said he was just fine.
Then we talked about her life. She worked as a waitress in a small café in the
center of her small town. She made just enough money to get by. She had
no friends to speak of, but the more we talked I got to be very fond of her,

and by the time we said goodbye I thought I might be in love with her. We met again the next day when she got out of work and I was swooning in her presence. We kissed and that was it, I fell head over heels for her. She said, "I barely know you." I said, "That's all right, you will." And by the end of that night, we were definitely in love, like two birds. Or two butterflies caught in the wind, not knowing where they were going. Just happy to be anywhere at all.

THE PHONE CALL

I sat on the steps for a very long time. No one passed, no cars went by.
It was as if the world had stopped. Then the mailman walked by. I was
so happy to see him I nearly jumped out of my pants. "Hi!" I shouted to him.
"Hello," he answered back. "How are you today?" I said. "I'm just fine. How
are you?" he said. "Well, I was a bit lonely until I saw you," I said.
"There's no reason to be lonely. There's all the world to keep you company,"
he said. "I guess you're right," I said, as he disappeared down the block.
Then school got out and the streets were flooded with youngsters. They were
sweet and friendly. A while later work ended and the grown-ups came home. They
were exhausted and not so friendly, but, still, they reminded me that there
was a world out there. I sat on the steps all that time, thinking about
what a funny place we live in. Then I got up and went in the house. I had
lost my job at the oil refinery and was waiting to hear from several other
companies. I had some savings and wasn't too worried. Jack called and
asked if I wanted to go hunting tomorrow. I said I'd like to but I had other
plans. Then Betsy called and asked if I wanted to go drinking tonight. I
said that sounded great, but I just couldn't. I waited for the phone to ring
after that, but there was nothing. I played some crossword puzzles, then
watched television and fell asleep on the couch. I woke up in the morning
feeling achy and lost. I wasn't sure where I was. It took me a few minutes
to figure it out. I was home, as always. I shaved and ate breakfast.
My mother called and I said I was just fine. It was a lie, of course, but
the truth would hurt her more. I wanted to go for a walk, but I was afraid
of missing a phone call. Finally the phone rang. The voice said, "Hello,

my name is Mark Smith and I'd like to offer you a job as president of Prudential Banks, the largest bank in America. Are you interested?" "Well, yes, but why me?" I said. "We want someone with no experience and no ideas about banking, and you seemed ideal," he said. "Why would you want someone like that?" I said. "We want to kill him," he said. "I don't think I'm interested," I said. "It's a great salary, nice vacations," he said. "No thanks," I said, feeling relieved and very lucky to be just where I am.

ELVIS HAS LEFT THE HOUSE

The raccoon got up on the roof and wouldn't come down. I threw rocks
at it and it danced between them. Finally I decided to get my shotgun.
I got a ladder from the garage and climbed up on it. Then I took aim and
fired. It danced like crazy, but I missed and tore a hole in the roof.
Denny, the little boy from next door, came running out of his house yelling,
"Don't shoot, that's my pet raccoon!" I turned on the ladder and stared at
him in disbelief. "All right, you can have him if you can catch him," I
said. He stood at the foot of the ladder and said, "Come here, Billy." And
to my amazement, the raccoon came down and nestled in his arms and they walked
away towards Denny's home. I put the ladder away and walked into my house
with my shotgun. I went into my study and started to work for a while.
I finished a report for work in about three hours, then decided to take
a nap. I went into the living room and lay down on the couch. I slept for
about an hour and when I woke up the raccoon was in my lap. I started to scream
but then thought better of it and just started to pet its head, which it seemed
to like. So we lay there like that for another half hour until there was a
knock on the door. I picked the raccoon up and walked to the door. It was
Denny, the boy from next door. "Can I have my raccoon back?" he said. "I
don't know how he got in here, really I don't. But, sure, here's your
raccoon," I said. "By the way, what's his name?" "Elvis," he said, grabbing
his pet. A few days later I had worked hard in the yard all day and was
tired. I went to bed early and when I woke up Elvis was in my arms. It
felt natural and good and I kissed him, which he seemed to like.
I got up and fixed him breakfast, which was cereal and milk. He liked that.

Then I went about my day and Elvis followed me around. He stayed that night. And the next night. In fact he seemed to be a permanent tenant by now. We had our routines and our meals. We slept together. One day when I was raking leaves in the fall I saw Bob and Susan in their yard. They were Dennis's parents. After we exchanged greetings and talked for a little bit, I said, "How's Denny?" "We thought you knew. Denny died last summer. It was polio," Bob said. "Oh, I'm so sorry. He'll be greatly missed, I know," I said. Then I finished raking and went back in the house. I did some paperwork, napped for a while, and fixed dinner. Something was different. Elvis wasn't there. I looked everywhere, but there was no Elvis.

A SHIFT IN THE ATTIC

I was swinging on the porch when all of a sudden I fell over
and hit the floor. I don't know how it happened, but I stood up and
brushed myself off. I stood there for a minute, dazed, and felt myself all over
to see if I was hurt. I seemed to be all right. I tested the swing to see
if it was broken, but it wasn't. Maybe it was an earthquake. I walked into
the kitchen and a teacup fell on my head. I thought that was mighty
strange. I swept it up. I went back into the living room and sat down
on the couch. I picked up the newspaper and read about a little girl who
fell into a hole and was never seen again. It made me sad. How could
that happen? There's an end to everything. My couch was sagging. I'm
going to hit the floor, I thought. And then I did. I got up and looked around.
This wasn't my house at all. Yes, it was. There was the little penguin
on the wall, and the walrus beside him. I recognized everything, down
to the little worm on the floor. I moved to the chair beside the window
where the light would be better. Now I could see my hand, not that I wanted
to. It was all gnarly and gray. The chandelier was shaking. Then suddenly all
was quiet. My hands were glowing and so were my cheeks. I felt healthy and
wise. I looked over at the staircase to the attic and there stood a moose.
I nearly jumped out of my skin. But the moose was calm, just looking
around. He walked over to me. There was a bowl of cookies on the table
and I started feeding them to him. He seemed to really like them. When
they were all gone, I walked into the kitchen. He followed me. I
opened the refrigerator and grabbed a head of lettuce and started to feed
it to him. When that was gone I gave him a bowl of spinach, and so on.

We were becoming great friends. Finally, there was a knock on the door. A man stood there and said, "That's my moose." I said, "No, it isn't. It's my moose." He was really mad. He said, "It isn't your moose. It's mine." "I swear it's mine," I said. And while we were arguing, the moose walked out onto the porch, jumped the rail and was gone, never to be seen again.

THE EXECUTION

The potboiler came back into the cave and said, "There are no rabbits anywhere today. I guess we'll have to slaughter one of our pigs, precious though they may be." "We can't do that. We'll never find a pig again. They are a dying species," Ham said. "But what are we going to eat? If there are no rabbits, we have no choice but to slaughter the pig," Tree said. "We could eat Bob. He's no use to us," Samovar said. "That's a great idea. Bob does nothing but eat our rabbits. He never hunts, he brings us nothing to eat. His time is up," Ham said. "Let's go get him," Samovar said. And so they all gathered and went in search of Bob. When they found him asleep under the banyan tree, Potboiler said, "Wake up, Bob, it's your turn to feed us." Bob rubbed the sleep from his eyes and said, "What do you mean? I can't feed you. I have no food." "No, you don't understand. We want to eat you," Samovar said. "Don't be silly. You can't eat me. I am one of you," he said. "You contribute nothing," Ham said. "I'm a wit, I'm really quite funny," Bob said. "We're talking about victuals, you know, food," Potboiler said. "Well, I guess I'm on the slight side there," he said. "Therefore we're going to eat you," Samovar said. "Oh, I see, it's becoming quite clear now," Bob said. "Who's going to do the job is the only question," Ham said. "I'll do it. I never liked Bob anyway," Samovar said. "Thanks a lot," Bob said. "Well, it's true," he said. "Let's not break into petty scrabbling," Tree said. "That's true, this should be a dignified execution," Potboiler said. "Let's get on with it," Ham said. "Bring me the sword," said Samovar. "We only have a knife and fork," Potboiler said. "What kind of execution is that?" Samovar said.

"It's a dainty one," Ham said. "I don't like a dainty execution," said Samovar. "I think I do," said Bob. Potboiler said, "I have an idea, let's just each of us have a popsicle and call it quits." "Yeah, that's a good idea. Let's just have popsicles," Ham said. "Sounds great to me," said Bob.

THE SHEPHERD

Betsy fell out of an airplane one day and floated down into the trees.
She was alright except for a stick stuck between her toes. She stayed
in the trees for several days until she was rescued by a sheep farmer one
morning. He took her home and removed the stick between her toes and gave her
a hot toddy. She fell in love with him and they were soon married. She
made him soup every day, which he thanked her for as though it was the first
time he had tasted it. He asked about her family and she said she had none.
She asked about his and he said he had many, though he said he never saw
them. She asked him why, and he said, "Sheep." Harold smoked his pipe most
of the day. When she asked him why he smoked it, he said, "Sheep." It
was the same answer he gave to everything. But he loved Betsy. You could tell
that by the way he wrapped the blanket around her in the evening. He never
wanted her to be cold, especially at night. He would build a fire and make
her sit by it every night. Then he would sing to her, the gentlest lullabies.
She would fall asleep like this every night. In the morning it was different.
He was all business, feed the sheep and water them, clean out their cages.
It was a long day's work. A break for lunch and little else. But when he
came home from work he always asked how she was, how her day had gone. And
she always told him it was fine. She asked him if he ever took vacation.
He said he had never thought about it. Who would take care of the sheep?
She said he could hire someone. Surely there was someone with that talent.
He said he would look into it. A week later he said he had found someone.
And so they took a trip to North Dakota a month later. They had rented a
cabin on a lake. Betsy loved it. They fished all day and cooked what they

caught on an open fire at night. Harold had never been so happy. When it was over they returned home, but the sheep were gone. They couldn't believe it. They searched everywhere, but they were gone. The man they had hired was a thief. What would they do now with no animals to tend to? They decided they would be happy without them. They would be poor, but happy. And if they ever caught up with the thief they would thank him. And then Harold would kill him.

THE LIAR

Earl and I were sitting around at my house one night when he said to me, "You know that story that's been going around about me shooting a deer through the heart with my bow and arrow? Well, it isn't true, I missed him altogether. I just made that up. Can you believe that?" "I guess so," I said. "And that four-pound bass I caught up at Lake Wyola was totally fake. I never even caught a fish that day," he said. "You don't have to be telling me all this. I still love you," I said. "And that 300-point bowling game I said I bowled last Christmas was more like 100, can you believe that? I lied just to make it more exciting," he said. "People do things like that all the time," I said. "I know, but I'm a chronic liar," he said. "You're just like everybody else. Don't worry about it," I said. "But I do. The truth should matter. We should stand for something real," he said. "Stop worrying about it. Nobody cares. You make life exciting, that's all that matters," I said. "Okay, if you say so, but I'm going to try to be better," he said. I got up and fixed us a drink. Earl leaned back and seemed to be enjoying himself now. "You're a great guy, you know that, Jethro. I can relax around you, be myself," he said. "Thank you, Earl. That's what friends should do for one another," I said. "Yes, sir, no putting on, no tall tales, just relaxing and being yourself." We sat there in silence for a while, sipping our drinks. "Say, have you ever climbed Mount Greylock?" he said. "No, I haven't," I said. "Well, I have. It was a bitch, nearly killed myself," he said. "Why was that?" I said. "The ledge was so steep, nearly straight down. If you slipped an inch it was straight down and you'd fall," he said. "How did you make it?" I said. "I didn't, I fell straight down and killed myself," he said. "That's a shame," I said. "You're telling me," he said.

MAGIC

I saw a child fall from a tree. I ran over to him, but when I got
there, he wasn't there. I looked all around, but I couldn't find him.
Finally I looked up at the treehouse and I saw him sitting there drinking
a can of soda. I climbed up to the treehouse and said, "I thought you
fell." He said, "I did, but I bounced back up." "I don't understand,"
I said. "It's easy. Magic," he said. "I don't know." "I don't understand
it myself," he said. "Well, explain what you do understand," I said.
"Well, before something really bad happens to me I just say, Oh my gosh,
oh my golly, Jesus Christ I'm coming home," he said. "So it's a Christian
thing," I said. "A what?" he said. "A Christian thing. You believe in
Christ," I said. "I don't know anything about that. It's just something
I say," he said. "What if you said it backwards?" I said. "I don't think
it'd work," he said. "Well, let's try it," I said. "I don't want to," he
said. "Why not?" I said. "Well, for one thing, I told you even when I say
it the other way around I only say it when I'm in an accident," he
said. "How about if I push you out of the treehouse?" I said. "If I agreed
to it then it wouldn't be an accident," he said. "You're right. You've
got me there. Just promise that the next time something happens to you
you'll say it backwards," I said. "Okay," he said. About an hour later when
we were playing a game of dominos I surprised him by tripping him when he
got up to get a cracker and he fell out of the treehouse. I heard him say,
"Jesus Christ, oh my gosh, oh my golly," and he shot straight up into the sky.
I waited for him to come down, but he didn't. I waited until nightfall, then
I went back to my own house, not without a great deal of sadness. I went
to the treehouse in the morning, feeling sick to my stomach at what I had
caused. I waited all day, then once again went home when night fell. The

same happened the next day. Then on the third day when I arrived I found Jason hard at work on a puzzle. I said, "Jason, where have you been?" He said, "Me? I've been asleep." "Where?" I said. "In my bedroom, of course," he said.

OUT OF BREATH

I sat in my office thinking: What would one do if one were me?
I couldn't come up with an answer, so I thought: What would one do if one were Julia?
That wasn't much easier. What would one do if one were Paul? And so on
down the line. Finally, I said, what would one do if one were Max? Oh yes,
Maximillian Dupree. I would shoot myself out of this mess. I would grab
a gun and start firing at anything that moved. No, I wouldn't. I would
be still, quiet as a mouse, and look over my shoulder to make sure nobody else
was moving. Then I'd fall asleep. When I woke up, no one was around.
The office was closed. I went into my boss's office and snooped around.
I couldn't find anything on me, no mention of my name anywhere. It was
strange, as if I never did anything at all. It made me want to quit. I grabbed
my keys and made for the door. I tried every key I had and none worked.
I went back in the boss's office and searched for some keys. I found one
and went back to the door. Thank God it worked. I let myself out and tried
the elevator. It wasn't working, so I tried the stairs instead. It was
twenty-seven floors down. When I reached the bottom I was out of breath.
I got onto the street around 7:30. I sat down on the first bench I saw under an
elm in the park across the street from our building. I was so out of
breath. I tried to calm down. Within fifteen minutes I was myself again.
Then I got up and tried to catch a bus, but they were all too crowded.
So I started to walk. A car stopped and offered me a ride. The driver looked
vaguely familiar. He called me by name. I looked closer. He was my son.
"Jacob," I said, "I almost didn't recognize you!" "That's because I'm made up
for a play. It's called *This Is Your Life*," he said. "Whose life is it?"

I said. "That's the trouble, nobody knows," he said. "Oh, I see," I said. "No you don't. I told you, nobody knows," he said. "Stop the car. Let me out of this car. You're not my son. My son would never say a thing like that," I said. "Well, you're not my father. Get out of this car," he said.

THE THIEF

My wife and I were spending a quiet night at home. She was reading a magazine on the couch and I was reading my novel in my chair. I said, "Darling, can I fix you a cup of hot chocolate?" She said, "That would be great." So I got up and went into the kitchen and started to boil the milk. A few minutes later I handed her the cup. "Hmmm, smells great. Thank you, darling," she said. I sat down and resumed my reading. She said, "Did you know a tiger has the same number of bones in it as a monkey?" "I don't believe it," I said. "And a whale has the same number as a mouse." "Get out of here," I said. "These are some little-known facts discovered by a man named John D. Baxter," she said. "He must be crazy," I said. Then we were quiet for a while. I looked over and she was asleep. I went on reading my novel. Then I put my novel down and got up and started to tiptoe around the house. I went into our bedroom and over to the dresser. I opened up Mitzy's jewelry box and let the jewels run through my fingers. There were some fantastic pieces in there, diamonds, rubies, emeralds. I thought about stealing some, but felt creepy about it. I put them back in the box and tiptoed back into the living room. I tripped on the coffee table and went crashing down. Mitzy woke with a start. "Go back to sleep," I said. "What was that?" she said. "I tripped, that's all," I said. She started to get up. "Where are you going?" I said. "I want to look in my jewelry box," she said. "Why?" I said. "I dreamed somebody was trying to steal something in there," she said. She went into the bedroom and looked in the box, then came out. "It's okay," she said. "Well, I'm glad," I said. She got back on the couch and picked up her magazine. "Did you know jellyfish have bigger brains than humans?" she said. "I don't believe it," I said. "Well, they do. It says right here," she said.

THE WALK HOME

I told the doctor I wouldn't be seeing him again. "No, I guess you won't," he said. I walked out the door feeling really good. Of course I knew I was going to die, but still the day looked bright to me. I walked down to the water. Ducks were circling around and about. A sailboat sailed by. I walked along the shore. The sun beat down on me. I felt as though I might live forever. I sat down on a bench and watched the joggers pass. A pretty blonde walked by and I said, "Hello." She looked at me and said hello. A man with a greyhound on a leash walked by. I got up and started to walk. A woodpecker was pounding on a tree. An airplane flew over, leaving a thick trail of smoke. I left the lake and walked on up the road. I crossed at the streetlights and crossed the bridge. A car swerved to miss me. I thought, that could have been it, the end right there, but I walked on, bravely dodging the cars. When I got to the residential district, I felt relieved. There were large elms and maples overhanging the street, and people pushing baby carriages. Dogs ran loose everywhere. A man stopped me and asked if I knew where 347 Walnut Street was. I said I didn't. He said, "Oh well, it didn't matter anyway." I said, "Why?" He said it was a funeral notice. I walked on, bumping into a fat lady with a load of groceries. I said I was sorry. She kept going, dropping a load of grapefruit. Then, further on, there was a giant explosion across the street. Police and firemen were there right away. It appears it was a gas main beneath the shop. No one was there, luckily, but the firetrucks had their hands full. I left before it was out. The shop was pretty much destroyed. When I got home I was tired. I made myself a cup of tea and sat down on the couch. I thought about calling my mother, but she was in heaven. I called her anyway. "Mom, how are you doing?" I said. "I'm bored. Don't come here. There's nothing to do," she said. "Aren't there angels?" I said. "Yes, but they're boring," she said. "But I was going to come see you," I said. "Go to hell, it's more exciting," she said. I had fallen asleep with my teacup in my hand. When I awoke I realized I had thought it was a phone. My mother would never be so sarcastic about heaven.

SECOND CHILDHOOD

Jody and I were sitting in the living room. I said, "You know, we haven't played miniature golf in twenty years." She said, "So what? I haven't had a popsicle in thirty years, and I'm still going." I said, "Yeah, and I haven't been to a zoo in God knows how long and I'm alright with that." "I haven't been bowling in ages," she said. "I haven't been to a baseball game since I can remember," I said. "What are we going to do?" she said. "It seems we're busy all the time," I said. "But what are we doing? All the things we used to love have disappeared," she said. "They're replaced by other things. The second half of our lives are just different," I said. "I think I liked the first half better," she said. "Don't say that. We're more productive now, I think," I said. Jody got up and looked out the window. "We're slowing down, like we're preparing for death," she said. "You're crazy. I'm working harder than ever before," I said. "Okay, let's drop the subject. We disagree, is that so bad?" she said. "What's for supper?" I said. "I haven't thought that far ahead. I guess I should," she said. "Let's go to the baseball game. We haven't been in forever. We can get a hot dog there. What do you say? It will be fun," I said. "Okay, it will certainly be different," she said. So, around six o'clock, we drove down to the stadium, bought our tickets, and found our seats. It was exciting. When the game started I felt a real childish rush, and I think Jody did, too. Around the third inning we hailed the hot dog man and got our meal. I felt like a kid sitting there watching the game and eating our hot dogs. Our team was ahead, 4 to 3. Then, in the bottom of the 7th, a ball was hit foul in our direction, and Jody was hit

in the head. She was knocked out and an ambulance was called. I rode
in the back with her to the hospital, holding her hand, which was limp.
When they pulled her into the operating room they told me to stay outside.
After about a half an hour the doctor came out to tell me she was dead.
I broke down crying and couldn't stop. A nurse came out to hold me.
I thought, this is how we relive our youth.

THE ARGONAUT

What made anyone think I was a Communist I don't know. I never went to any of the Communist meetings. I didn't know any other Communists. I didn't believe in any of their tenets. It's true, I hunted elk in the winter. I never actually shot any, but I followed them. And I laced my cranberry juice with vodka. But these things didn't make me a Communist. I stood on the bridge and watched the boats go out to sea. I dreamed of going with them one day. I danced alone in my apartment. I hated my job with the government. I went to parties where I didn't know anyone. I went to the zoo and talked to the animals. I dreamed I had an affair with a zebra and its stripes rubbed off on me. I met a woman I liked and called her on the phone. She said she liked phone sex and I didn't know what she meant. I lay on the couch and counted my blessings. There were none, or so few they slipped through my fingers. I got up and looked out the window. A cloud of sparrows flew by. I made myself a can of soup. I thought of my relatives, all gone except for one. I called her on the phone. She didn't remember me. I told her I was Edna's son. She said, "I remember Edna. I never liked her. She cursed too much." My mother never cursed, but I wasn't about to argue. I went to the movies. I saw Hopalong Cassidy. I wished he didn't wave so much. But I liked the popcorn. I walked about the city, feeding the pigeons. I bought a soda on the street. I sat down in a garden. A woman came along and sat down beside me. She said, "Nice day, isn't it?" I said, "Yes, very, I like it." "What do you do for a living?" she said. "I'm an accountant in the government," I said. "That must be nice," she said. "But most people I know think I'm a Communist," I said. "That's a joke, right?" she said. "To me it is," I said. "To me, you look more like an Argonaut," she said. "What's an Argonaut?" I said. "It's somebody who swims in the deep waters of the ocean in search of treasure," she said. "I found a penny in my bathtub once when I was a kid," I said. "Then you're an Argonaut," she said.

THE FLOORPLAN TO HEAVEN

I was asleep on my desk when the boss walked in. I woke immediately and said, "I was just looking for a paper clip that seemed to escape here." "Who cares about a paper clip? I know I don't." "I was just thinking about the money. Paper clips cost plenty and I thought it might save the company," I said. "Paper clips cost nothing and I'm paying you a good salary to build shopping malls. Now let's stop this nonsense. Get to work now," he said, and left in a huff. I sat up straight and tried to remember what I was supposed to do. Oh, yes, Macy's. The floorplan. After work I was going to meet Eleanor for a drink at Lefty's. Eleanor was beautiful and smart. Maybe afterwards we could go to my place. Another drink and then some dinner. I could cook up my special pasta. Some music. And then to bed. That would be lovely. But she's not that kind of girl. It's only our second date. Be happy with that. Maybe talk about opera, not baseball. But I don't know anything about opera. Maybe she likes baseball or boxing. You never know with a girl like that. The boss said, "Larry, are you almost through?" "Oh, yes, just give me a few more minutes," I said. I hate this job. I really do. It's impossible to carry on a straight line of thinking without some interruption. Maybe I could get a job in a lighthouse, look for submarines all day. Macy's. What do I care about Macy's. And, yet, my life depends on it. I can't even remember what it is I am supposed to do. Deconstruct the Parthenon. Make the Acropolis out of Lincoln Logs. Make Eleanor out of fire.

THE SHADOWS OF
THE TREES ON THE WATER

The old apple tree was struck down by lightning a year
ago today. My grandfather had planted it shortly after he
built this house. We had apple pie every year of my life.
But life moves on. Now Cindy goes to the store and buys us
a cherry pie every now and then. I like cherry pie. But
Cindy's changed. I don't really know her anymore. She's
depressed most of the time. Stays in bed. Sometimes she
cries. I try to cheer her up. I tell her jokes. One day
I took her for a walk. I told her stories of my childhood,
which was pretty awful. How my older brother used to beat me
just for laughs and my father used to cheer him on. But
mostly she just sits there staring into space. I leave her
alone for days. I try to feed her, a spoonful of porridge
at a time. She spits it up on me and I go on feeding her.
It's a thankless job, really. Then one morning she wakes up
and says, "Let's go to the park today." I say, "Really?
Are you sure you feel up to it?" She says, "Sure. It's a
beautiful day. The park would be lovely." So we go. When
we get there Cindy wants to rent a boat and go out on the
lake. We do that and she insists on paddling. When we get
to the middle of the lake she stops paddling. She says, "Isn't
it lovely here?" I say, "Oh yes, the ducks are beautiful."
"And the shadows of the trees on the water," she says. We

sit there in silence for a while. Then a hawk flies over. "Look," I say. But she doesn't. I look at her. She's slumped over. I quickly step towards her, kneel down, feel her pulse. She's dead. I can't believe it, but it's true. I try breathing into her mouth. I pump her heart. Nothing works. I lean over and embrace her. "Cindy, Cindy," I cry, "why have you forsaken me?" Then I toss her overboard into the lake.

TRANSPARENT CHILD

As for the ghost, he was never seen again. My wife and
I settled into our new house. Actually it was a very old house,
with a feeling of unease. Every squeak was analyzed and dissected.
Nothing went unnoticed. When Julianna went to the bathroom, I thought
I saw him dart from room to room, but it was only a lace curtain
swaying in the wind. There were numerous mis-sightings like that.
But the first one was unmistakable. Julianna and I were sitting
in the living room having a nice chat about our new home when this
ghost appeared in the doorway and stood staring at us for what
felt like a minute. We were both shaking and speechless. It's
hard to describe him, really. I guess he looked like a ghost.
He didn't speak, just stared at us. And then he was gone. But
it was a ghost, all right, of that I am sure. But over the next week
or so we continued to unpack. There was so much to do. We met
our neighbors. They brought us a cake. We went to the grocery
store. We cooked dinner. We finally felt like we were settled in.
So I went back to work. I came home at night and there was
the paper. Then dinner and talk about how the job was going. And
problems with the house, the gutters and the shutters. And when
we would have children. Oh yes, that was no small thing. Julianna
wanted them now, but I said we'd have to wait until we were more
financially secure. She said that was an excuse that could be
used forever. I said we could barely afford our new mortgage.
And on and on the argument went. In fact, it went on for more than

a year. Then one day she told me she was pregnant. I pretended to be happy. But as the birth grew closer my excitement grew. We made lists of names. We bought clothes and toys. We decorated the room. And then one day we rushed to the hospital and after hours of labor the baby was born. It was a boy, but so pale it looked like a ghost. I asked the doctor what was wrong with him. The doctor said, "Nothing's wrong with him. He's just a see-through baby."

THE DEAD MAN'S FRIEND

An old man was sitting on a bench outside the courthouse.
When I walked by he said, "Hey, young fellow, can you spare a dime?"
I reached in my pocket and the next thing you know he had toppled over.
I thought maybe he was joking, but he stayed like that for a while.
I walked up to him and felt his pulse. There wasn't any. I stood
there for a minute, unsure of what to do next. Somebody came out
of the courthouse and I told him there was a dead man on the bench.
He looked at his watch and said, "I'm in a hurry." I saw a police-
man standing on the corner directing traffic. I ran the half a
block up to him and said, "Excuse me, Officer, but there's a man
who died just down the street. Could you please come and help
me?" "Can't you see I'm in charge of traffic flow at this busy
intersection?" he said. I threw up my arms and ran back to stand
by my man. I stood there for a few moments wringing my hands. Then
I ran up the stairs to the courthouse. I stopped the first person
I saw who looked like he worked there. "Could you please help me?
A man has died right outside on a bench and I need someone to take
him from me." "See the man in the next office," he said and walked
away. I walked into the next office and the man at the desk said,
"Can I help you?" I said, "Yes, there's a dead man right outside
this building. Can you arrange to have him moved?" "Fill out these
forms and the man in the next office will see you," he said. I
took the forms and sat down outside his office. I didn't know the
answers to any of the questions. What is the deceased's name? His

address? His age? Nearest of kin and so on. I threw the forms in the trash and walked out of the building. I sat down on the bench next to the dead man. "No one wants you," I said. "What are we going to do?" Then, after a few minutes, standing up, I said, "Come on, old man, let's go home."

MY FATHER AND ME

A man called me today and said he was my father. I said, "That's nice, but my father is dead." He said, "Well, I'm back and I just wanted you to know if you need anything I'll be there for you." He gave me his number and said goodbye. I hated that phone call because it upset me a great deal. My father had died when I was a small child. I didn't even remember him. But my mother had told me how brave he was, how kind and good. Now this impostor was causing me to acknowledge how little I really knew. But I couldn't get him out of my mind. He didn't deny he had been dead, he just said he was back. I went to work as usual. I met with friends. I didn't say anything to any of them. I let two weeks pass before I couldn't stand it any longer. Then I finally called the number he had given me. He answered and we set a date for the next night. We met in a bar near where I lived. He asked me what I did for a living. I told him I was an accountant. Then he asked me if I had any girlfriends. I said a few. We sat there in silence for a while. I asked if he had lived around here for long. He said, "Not long." I asked where he had lived. He said, "Oh, here and there." He asked me how my mother was. I said, "She's fine. She doesn't get around much anymore, you know." At some point in the conversation I reached over and touched his sleeve. His left arm began to crumble, slowly, before my eyes. It was like some magic trick, but it wasn't a trick. I could see that. His arm was completely gone now. Then I touched his other arm. The same thing happened.

The slow crumble, the disappearance. He kept on talking, mostly about me. Then I touched his leg, first one, then the other. Then his chest, until he was only a head talking. That's when he said, "You're my only son, after all, and I wouldn't want anything to happen to you."

THE GOVERNMENT LAKE

The way to the toy store was blocked by a fallen tree
in the road. There was a policeman directing traffic down a
side street. I asked him, "What happened?" He said, "Lightning
in the night." I took the turn and drove down the street
looking for a way to turn back. Other streets were blocked by
fallen trees, and I couldn't find a way back to the toy store.
I kept driving and soon I was on the outskirts of town. I
got on a highway and drove, soon forgetting the toy store and
what I was supposed to get there. I drove on as if I was hypno-
tized, not noticing the signs for turnoffs. I must have driven
a couple of hours before I woke up, then I took the next exit
and had no idea where I was. I drove down a straight treelined
lane with farmhouses on either side. There was a lake at the
end of the lane. I pulled over and parked. I got out and
started walking. There were several docks along the shore.
I walked out on one and watched the ducks swimming and diving.
There was something bobbing in the middle of the lake. I stared
at it for a long time before I realized it was a man's head.
Then, a moment later, it was a coconut. No, it was an old tire
floating right side up. I gave up and started following the
ducks. They would suddenly fly up and circle the lake and
come down and splash-land again. It was quite entertaining.
A man walked up behind me and said, "This government lake is
off-limits to the public. You'll have to leave." I said,

"I didn't know it was a government lake. Why should it be off-limits?" He said, "I'm sorry. You'll have to leave." "I don't even know where I am," I said. "You'll still have to leave," he said. "What about that man out there?" I said, pointing to the tire. "He's dead," he said. "No, he's not. I just saw him move his arm," I said. He removed his pistol from his holster and fired a shot. "Now he's dead," he said.

THE DEVIL

I was digging through some papers in my desk drawer
when I came across a ceramic figure that seemed quite old.
It was a devil of some sort, possibly Aztec. I don't remember
where I got it. Maybe it was a gift. Anyway, I took it out
and put it up on the shelf in the living room. I liked it
there. When my girlfriend, Cecilia, came over a couple of
nights later, she spotted it immediately. "That's mine,"
she said. "Well, what am I doing with it?" I said. "You
stole it," she said. "Why would I steal it?" I said. "You
liked it and wanted it for your own," she said. "I just
found it in the back of my desk drawer," I said. "You were
hiding it from me," she said. "I told you, I don't know how
it got there," I said. "Well, I want it back," she said.
"Fine, take it, it's yours," I said. "I will, thank you,"
she said. So she took it back and placed it on her mantel
and we didn't mention it for some time. Then one day when she's
over at my place she says, "What are you doing with my devil?"
I said, "What devil?" She said, "The one right there," pointing
to it on my desk. "I swear I don't know. I didn't take it,"
I said. "Yes you did. Admit it," she said. "I haven't seen it
since it was over at your place," I said. "You're a liar,"
she said. "No, that's the truth," I said. I gave it back
to her and said I didn't want to see it again. The next time
I was over at her place I quietly looked around. I didn't

spot the devil anyplace. Finally, I said, "Where'd you put the devil?" "Oh, I threw it away," she said. "You what?" I said. "I threw it away. It was just too much trouble, I mean, between us," she said. I was sad, I missed it. I had grown very fond of it. But I didn't say anything. When I got home that night, I looked around. Surely it was some-place. Finally, I went to bed. In the middle of the night something woke me. It was the devil, only it was an angel, and it said, "Get rid of her. She'll hurt you. She's a fallen one." I reached out to touch him, but he was gone.

TOO LATE

There wasn't much I could do. I sat there looking out
the window. A squirrel was digging for what he hoped was a
nut. Several flickers were jumping about in the yard. I
looked at my watch. It was 11:23 a.m. Nobody did much
at that hour. I don't know why I said that, just because
I wasn't doing anything. Other people were making bombs,
sending love letters. Or just doing their jobs, whatever
that might be. I was waiting for a sign so that I might
proceed with my . . . my . . . whatever it is I'm supposed to do.
A man walked down the street looking suspicious. I watched
him until he disappeared. Who was he? Was he the sign I
was waiting for? I don't know. Sparrows were flitting about.
A chipmunk ran across the road. And I am still waiting, as if
for a sign from God. Jonquils blossoming in the side yard.
I was beginning to feel like a prisoner. I couldn't leave,
not with so much at stake. There was a light knocking
on the front door. I went to answer it. There was a beautiful woman
standing there. "Yes?" I said. "I have a message for you.
Can I come in?" she said. "Of course," I said. I took her
into the living room. "Have a seat," I said. "Do you know why
I'm here?" she said. "I have no idea, I mean, I might, but
I'm still not sure," I said. "Well, it's your time. Do you
know what that means?" she said. "Not exactly," I said.
"You're Number One," she said. "What does that mean?" I said.

"It means you can do anything you want right now," she said. "Oh what a relief. I thought it meant I was going to die," I said. "So what do you want to do?" "Let me think about it," I said. We sat there in silence for a while. Then I said, "I guess I'm just happy sitting here." "That's it. You don't want anything. Great. Okay, I'll see you around," she said, getting up and heading for the door. "Well, maybe a kiss would be nice," I said. "Too late," she said, slamming the door.

THE PRAYER

My dog came back from the woods smelling of skunk, so
I gave him a good wash in the tub outside and things were
better. We took a walk down the street and met another dog,
a big one. They snarled at one another and then made their
peace. After a good walk we turned around and went back
home. Robbie, the dog, went to sleep in his corner, and I
did some paperwork. I was going along just fine until there
was a knock on the door. I answered it and it was my ex-wife.
She said she had come for the dog and I said that wasn't in
the agreement. She said she had bought the dog and it was
hers. I said Robbie loved me. She said a dog doesn't know
what love is. "This is the dog's home, his neighborhood," I
said. "He'll adapt to his new home in a day," she said.
"You don't give this dog real feelings about anything," I
said. "He's a dog, for Christ's sake," she said. "He's my dog.
He comes when I call him, he sits when I tell him to, he
fetches, he sleeps when I sleep. We're like married to each
other," I said. "And now he wants to divorce you," she said.
"He does not. We're happy together," I said. "Well, we'll
be happy together, too," she said. "It would break his heart
to leave me," I said. "You don't know what you're talking
about," she said. I called Robbie. He didn't come. I called
him again. "Where's your dog now?" she said. "I'll get
him," I said. I went and looked in the bedroom. He wasn't

there. I looked in the study. He wasn't there either. I went in the guest bedroom. He wasn't there. I came back into the living room. "I can't find him," I said. "He's got to be someplace," she said. "You didn't let him out when you came in, did you?" I said. "Definitely not," she said. "Well, I can't find him in the house," I said. "Robbie!" she called, "Robbie!" He wasn't anywhere. "What are we going to do?" I said. "Let's pray," she said. "What?" I said. "Let's pray for Robbie to come back, it can't hurt," she said. "Okay, if you think it might help," I said. We closed our eyes and held hands. "Heavenly Father, please bring our Robbie safely back to us," she said. We opened our eyes and there was a camel standing there. "Oh, no, you've made a mistake," I said. "I didn't make a mistake. God did," she said. "Come here, Robbie," I said. And the huge animal stepped nearer and rubbed his snout on my shoulder just like Robbie always did when he wanted to express his affection for me. "He's half yours," I said.

THE VISITING DOCTOR

This afternoon about half past four I was sitting at my desk when somebody knocked on my door. I got up to answer it when my leg crumbled beneath me. I tried to stand, but it was as if my one leg were made of silly putty. Finally, with the help of the arms of the couch, I pulled myself up and yelled at the door, "Come in, the door's unlocked." The door opened slowly and there stood a little man in a doctor's uniform. "You rang?" he said. "Well, not exactly," I said. "Yes, but you need me. Am I right?" he said. "Yes, I suppose I do," I said. "Well, then, let's get right to work. It's your left leg, am I right?" he said. "Yes, it's my left leg," I said. "Well, I'm afraid we'll have to saw it off," he said. "No, please don't. You haven't even looked at it," I said. "I heard you fall. I know the sound. It's no good anymore," he said. "It just went to sleep," I said. "Yes, forever, it went to sleep forever, and that's why we have to cut it off," he said. "No, not forever. It just went to sleep the moment I heard the door knock," I said. "Are you accusing me, because, if you are . . ." he said. "No, no, nothing like that. It's just a curious circumstance," I said. "Then put your leg on the table," he said. "I don't think I want to," I said. "We're not talking about want. It's a necessity," he said. "Who are you, anyway?" I said. "I'm your doctor," he said. "But I only just met you," I said. "And just in time," he said. "I want you to leave my house," I said. "But you are a sick man. You need help right now," he said. "My leg is beginning to wake up, I swear it is," I said. "You only wish it were. Stop this silliness and put your leg up on the table," he said. "Please leave this house right now, I beg you," I said. "Not without your leg I won't," he said. I picked up a lamp and crashed it down upon his head. He dropped to the floor unconscious. My leg was fine, back to its old self again. Then I picked him up and dragged him outside and dropped him in the gutter.

MARRIED TO THE WRONG MAN

I said I was very sorry for all the trouble I had caused
her. She said it was no trouble at all. I offered her a drink.
She said a drink would be nice. We sat down on the sofa. I
asked her her name again. She said, "Matilda, just like in
the song." I said, "I've never known a Matilda. That's a great
name." "My mother always wanted to go to Australia, but naming
me Matilda was as close as she got," she said. "Why did you
save me back there?" I said. "You looked like a good man," she
said. "Thank you. I just got my hair cut," I said. She laughed.
"I think I'd like you even without a haircut," she said. "That's
very generous of you," I said. "I just speak the truth," she
said. "Always?" I said. "No, just when I feel like it," she
said. "Oh, then I'll be careful," I said. "You don't have to,"
she said. "Why?" I said. "I told you, I like you," she said.
"Can I kiss you?" I said. "If you like," she said. So I kissed
her. And I kissed her some more. I kissed her until we were both
dizzy. "That was great," I said. "Don't stop," she said. Then
I took her to bed. We made love most of that night, and it was
joyous. When we woke in the morning there was a thunderstorm.
She said, "I have to go." I said, "Why? Wait until the storm is
over." She said, "I can't. I'm married." "Oh," I said, "that
makes a difference." "I'm sorry," she said, "I should have told
you." "I guess it wouldn't have happened then," I said. "Probably
not," she said. She reached in her purse and pulled out a revolver.

"And now I have to kill you. I'm sorry," she said. "I won't tell anyone what happened. I promise," I said. "It's not that. It's that if you're here I'll want to sleep with you again. I really like you and I can't risk that," she said. "Why don't you leave your husband?" I said. "I can't. We married for life, and, besides, he's immortal," she said. "He's what?" I said. "He's immortal. I know, I've tried to poison him three times and I shot him through the heart twice. It doesn't bother him," she said. "Also, he's terribly jealous and has a bad temper." "That's a shame, it really is, but you don't have to kill me. We can tell him we're just friends," I said. "But he knows when I lie to him," she said. "Okay, shoot me," I said. She aimed the pistol at my head, and then said, "I can't do it." "Why not?" I said. "Because I don't have any bullets," she said.

THE FINAL VACATION

Why was there no knob on the door? It was terribly hard
to get in. I had to gnaw it with my teeth. And once inside
there was no place to sit. This was a very strange vacation
home. Of course there was no food in the pantries. I didn't
expect any. But what would I do with no bed? Sleep on the
floor, I guess. There were two small windows in the house, about
a foot square, one in the kitchen and one in the bedroom,
both high up near the ceiling. They shed enough light during
the daytime. And at night I don't know what I am supposed to do.
Candles, I suppose, but I don't have any candles. One can
always sleep. So I put my things down on the floor and sat
down. I would be here for about a week. I started to think of
all the things I had left behind. No, I said, you mustn't do
that. And I would get lonely, nobody to talk to all those days.
Oh well, this was the vacation I had worked so hard for, I
wasn't going to waste it complaining. The first night I slept
like a baby, nothing woke me. When I woke in the morning I
felt refreshed and ready to go. The trouble was there was
no place to go. I needed food. Where was I to get it? Outside
there was a prairie as far as the eye could see, no shops or
stores. Why didn't they warn me? I walked around outside
hoping to get an idea. There wasn't a tree anywhere. I walked
around kicking the dust. I went back to the cabin. I was
going to starve for a week. I scratched around on the floor

for a while, then I fell asleep. When I woke it was dark out and I couldn't see a thing. I crawled around and bumped into things. There was no point in keeping a diary. Nothing much changed for the next seven days. I walked around in the daylight when I had the strength. I never did find anything to eat. I slept when it got dark. But this is the hard part to explain, I got to like it. The weaker my hunger made me, the more I thrived. I woke the seventh day and I wanted to hide out here forever. There was a knock on the door and a man said, "It's time to leave." I said, "No, please let me stay." "You can't break the rules, you must leave," he said. I raised my hand up as though to pray, and that's when it happened. I slowly disappeared into the darkness of the cabin, never to be seen again.

A DREAM COME TRUE

I was tired after work so when I got home I took a nap.
I slept for about an hour and when I got up I fixed dinner,
some hot dogs and beans. Then I was going to watch television,
but there was nothing on. So I picked up a book and started to
read. The book was about an Eskimo boy who is shot out of a cannon
and lands in Arkansas and becomes a highway patrolman. This seemed
promising. Then there was a knock at the door. I answered it and
a policeman was standing there. He said, "I'm sorry to bother
you, but there is a boy missing from down the block. I was wondering
if you had seen him." He showed me a picture of the boy. "No,
I've not seen him, that is to say, recently. Of course, I've seen
him, I think it was last summer," I said. "Well, if you catch sight
of him now please give us a call," he said, handing me his card.
"I certainly will," I said. I watched his car back out of the
drive, then went back to the couch. I sat there staring into space
for a while. I couldn't tell what was real and what was not. The
bookcase was like a giant mushroom swaying in a wind. The lamp
was a cornstalk whispering something obscene. I knew that boy.
I gave him Halloween candy every year. Well, that's not really
knowing him, but I felt that I did. I think he was about twelve,
his name was Bobby or Joey, something like that. I had put him
out of my mind. There were mouse droppings on the kitchen floor.
I had to do something about that. I remembered when I was twelve.
I thought about running away from home, not too seriously, but I

did. But this boy could be kidnapped. He could be murdered for all I know. He could be cut in little pieces and buried in . . . in my backyard! I was getting tired and went to bed. I woke up in the morning and fixed myself a cup of coffee. As I was sitting in the living room I realized with a start that Joey, or whatever the hell his name was, was sitting right across from me. I said, "What the hell are you doing here?" He said, "I always wanted to meet you like this. I thought you'd make a nice dad."

THE TRUTH

Mitzy fell asleep as soon as we got home, but I didn't.
The evening had upset me. Why did Jack keep asking me if I'd
been married before? And why did my answer not satisfy him?
It was probably just a bad joke. Jack's humor is off sometimes.
But he's not a bad guy. Well, then I went to bed. When we woke up
in the morning Mitzy said, "Jack was right about you, wasn't he?"
"What do you mean?" I said. "Jack said you were kicked out of
the army," she said. "I was never in the army, how could I be
kicked out?" I said. "I don't think he likes me." "Oh, I think
Jack likes you a lot. He just wishes you were more interesting,"
she said. "And by making me secretly divorced and secretly kicked
out of the army I'm instantly more interesting, is that it?" I
said. "According to Jack you are," she said. "I think we had better
have breakfast," I said. "Good idea," she said. During breakfast
I said, "Don't you think I'm interesting?" "Of course I do, honey,"
she said. "Let's forget it. I mean, Jack is an old friend. Maybe
he was just drunk," I said. "That's probably it," she said.
"What are you going to do today?" I asked. "I'm thinking of buying
a new dress for the wedding," she said. "What wedding?" I said.
"You know, Carol and Bob's wedding, next Saturday," she said.
"Oh God, I forgot all about it," I said. "How could you forget?
Bob's your best friend," she said. "I know, I just had my mind
on other things, but now I'll focus on their wedding, I promise,"
I said. Shortly after that Mitzy left the house. I cleaned up

the breakfast dishes, then sat down on the couch. Why had Jack told the two secrets I had told him years ago. I had sworn him to silence, and now everybody knew. I had told him I would kill him if he ever told anybody. I wasn't going to kill him, but I did think about disappearing, just vanishing altogether. Where would I go? What would I do? And I do love Mitzy. I could tell her the truth. I've had eighteen years to do that, and not a squeak so far.

I SAT AT MY DESK AND CONTEMPLATED ALL THAT I HAD ACCOMPLISHED

I sat at my desk and contemplated all that I had accomplished this year. I had won the hot dog eating contest on Rhode Island. No, I hadn't. I was just kidding. I was the arm wrestling champion in Portland, Maine. False. I caught the largest boa constrictor in Southern Brazil. In my dreams. I built the largest house out of matchsticks in all the United States. Wow! I caught a wolf by its tail. Yummy. I married the Princess of Monaco. Can you believe it? I fell off of Mount Everest. Ouch! I walked back up again. It was tiring. Snore. I set a record for sitting in my chair and snoring louder than anybody. Awake! I set a record for swimming from one end of my bath to the other in No Count, Nebraska. Blurb. I read a book written by a dove. Great! I slept in my chair all day and all night for thirty days. Whew! I ate a cheeseburger every day for a year. I never want to do that again. A trout bit me when I was washing the dishes. But I couldn't catch him. I flew over my hometown and didn't recognize anyone. That's how long it's been. A policeman stopped me on the street and said he was sorry. He was looking for someone who looked just like me. What are the chances?